I0530963

SNOWBELL

By Denise M. Baran-Unland

Illustrated by Christopher Gleason

SNOWBELL, Copyright © 2016 by Denise M. Baran-Unland.
All rights reserved.

PRINTED IN THE UNITED STATES OF AMERICA

This book is a work of fiction. Names, characters, businesses,
organizations, places, events, and incidents are the product of the
author's imagination. Any resemblance is purely coincidental.

No part of this book may be reproduced or transmitted by any
means, mechanical or electronic, including photocopying,
recording, or by any information storage and retrieval system,
without the written consent of the author. For more information,
contact BryonySeries@gmail.com

Cover art by Christopher Gleason
Cover design by Sarah Stegall
ISBN 978-0-9852748-4-9
www.bryonyseries.com

This book is lovingly dedicated to the reader, whoever you might be.

"Those who'll play with cats must expect to be scratched."
~ Miguel de Cervantes

The autumn rain splashed against the patio glass and trickled in silent streams to muddy pools near the sliding door. I stood unblinking and watched it, relieved for dry, cozy shelter, and yet wistful for the future my haughty recklessness had prematurely extinguished.

I closed my eyes and recalled another rainy day years ago when, sitting cross-legged in a circle on the cold tile floor of the kindergarten room, we answered our teacher's question, "What do you want to be when you grow up?"

Many of the replies included mommies, teachers, nurses, and stenographers, for this was nineteen fifty-eight and few girls in Grover's Park aspired to much more. I, however, had already visited Europe twice with my parents and was more intrigued with airline uniforms than with famous landmarks and old museums. I happily blurted, "Stewardess," but never in my most fanciful reveries did I imagine living out my days as a cat.

Looking back, the clues foreshadowing my destruction were everywhere, but how, then, was I to know they were harmful? All had logical explanations. The hypnotizing gray shadow flitting by an east, second floor mansion window was the result of a cloud passing near the sun. The leer from the short, faintly hunched businessman at Sue's Diner was merely the act of a dirty old man. The beckoning mist at the woods' edge around twilight was nothing more than cool water vapor, swirling as it met the day's humid air and condensed. To think I had once considered it provocative to hide behind the general store, necking and petting with the twenty-something lead singer from the centennial band!

At any point during my expedition into the woods I could have turned back, but there is something electrifying about roaming outdoors at night. Underneath the serenity of a starry sky, long after domesticated mortals have yawned and slunk to bed, another world of predatory creatures rises and begins their day. I'm not talking ghosts here, but ordinary beings: opossums, foxes, owls, and even bats. The alien sounds and shapes of the dark scared the other girls, but they enlivened me, and I ached to run free. Yet, even *I* wasn't foolish enough to enter a deteriorating building after midnight. I only planned to inhabit the grounds until dawn, the first person courageous enough in this hick little village to do it, and return with the triumphant report that the mansion's ghost legends were false.

It hadn't quite worked out that way.

I was blissfully tearing across the estate grounds, just past the ramshackle gazebo, when a shrill cry ripped into the night. Not a brief screech, such as one might hear from a barn owl, but a long, painful wail that escalated higher and higher until it ended in a bone-chilling shriek. I started, tripped, and smacked face down into a half-buried cobblestone. I lay, stunned, while the shock of the accident washed over me. My head throbbed, my skin smarted, and my limbs refused to move. I painfully sat up and gingerly shifted my arms and legs. Blood ran down my nose and trickled into my mouth. Great. My mother had been shopping my portfolio around, and three modeling agencies had already expressed interest. Worried, I sat on the damp ground for a long while and pressed my jacket sleeve across my face until the flow slowed. I briefly considered turning back, but pride intervened, for I simply refused to become another victim of a small town myth. So I pressed my palms on the ground to steady myself, slowly stood, and gathered my bearings. The gazebo was behind me, on the left, which meant the mansion had to be straight ahead. I took a hesitant step. It didn't hurt as much as I expected, but running was obviously no longer possible. What did it matter? I had all night. As I hobbled toward the mansion, I kept a sharp lookout. What had caused that awful sound?

Just as I rounded the front of the old house, there was a crunching of tires and a bright beam of light. Had the girls called the police? As my eyes adjusted to the scene, I saw the vehicle was not a squad car. The door opened, and a man in a long, dark coat emerged. I recognized him immediately. He was the businessman scrutinizing me yesterday afternoon. I edged away, preparing to bolt, if necessary, confident that, even in my condition, I could outrun someone as old as he.

"Good Lord!" The man stepped closer and adjusted his horn-rimmed glasses. "It's the little girl from Sue's Diner."

The term "little girl" rankled me, and I momentarily lost my mistrust of him. Most people considered me older than seventeen, even when I wasn't wearing makeup, and the fact that he hadn't tried to sound condescending made it worse.

"Sir, you are trespassing on private property," I said in my most preemptory tone. I was, after all, an official guest and had the authority to make pronouncements. "I could have you arrested."

He threw back his head and laughed heartily. Apparently, he was too stupid to understand the trouble I could cause for him. "Arrest me! Little girl, you do realize I sit on the village board?"

Before I recovered from this shock, he peered closer and said, "You're bleeding."

Still? I dabbed my hand against my nose. His tone had been flat, unconcerned. He had made an observation, nothing more. Well, I wasn't worried, either. "It's nothing."

"Nonsense." He took a step forward, "and look how swollen that hand is. I noticed you limping, too. What happened? Did someone hurt you?"

"No, I fell." He was forcing me to answer questions, and I didn't like it. I was losing control of the situation. I had to regain it, quickly, but how?. The older people back home were easier to dismiss. "It's nothing," I repeated, but my objection sounded hollow and empty.

"Little girl, do you realize you might have a concussion, whiplash, or even a hairline fracture in your neck?"

I was tired of the phrase, "little girl," and I tossed my head defiantly to prove both my chagrin and the fact that nothing was broken. "I'm sure I'm fine," I said, all the while considering the merits of walking away from the building until he left. I had no intentions of returning to the servant's cottage until morning, but how would *he* know that?

"Nevertheless," he said. "I recommend you go inside and allow me to dress those wounds before I take you home."

Go inside the mansion? With *him*? I remembered the smirking the way he had looked at Sue's Diner. Did he really think I was so naive? So what if he was a board member? Even if he could prove his mighty status, he certainly had no business on these grounds in the middle of the night. Technically, I didn't either, but I wasn't going to admit that. I shot a haughty, "I don't think so!" and started to limp away, but he stepped closer and laid a firm hand on my shoulder.

"I can't fix you up out here," he said with impatience.

I tried shaking him free, but he was obviously stronger than he looked. Instead, I looked at him with all the scorn I could muster. "I'm not going in there with you. Good night!"

"Look, you chit!"

He handed me a card, and I shuffled closer to the headlights to read it.

Dr. Abner Rothgard
Board certified in neurology,
hematology, immunology, cardiology,

endocrinology, obstetrics, and veterinary and internal medicine.

All right, so the man was no dummy, but I still felt cautious. What business would such a prestigious doctor have at the mansion and at this hour, too? I dropped the card and said, "If you're a really doctor, why are you at the estate in the middle of the night?" Somehow, my words lacked the bite I hoped they'd have.

Dr. Rothgard shut off the ignition, grabbed his medical bag, and slammed the door. "Really, I should be asking you that question."

"I'm staying at the servant's cottage for the weekend." I put my hands on my hips, cocked my head, and said, "Your turn," hoping he'd act just a little intimidated.

"Heavens, what an impertinent child! Since you must know, I was securing the building for the night."

This time, I ignored his slam on my youth. "You couldn't do that during normal hours? The tours ended hours ago."

"A hospital emergency prevented it." Dr. Rothgard shook his head in what seemed to be a regretful manner. "I won't force you to accept medical treatment, but as a doctor and village official, I do have to act. Therefore, I will simply contact the police and call for an ambulance. Good night." He turned toward his car.

"Wait!"

If he called the authorities, I would return as a laughingstock with my tail between my legs. I had never been humiliated, especially by an adult, and I had no intention of starting now. I thought fast. If I accepted his recommendation, I could afterwards pretend to go back, hide amongst the trees until he departed, and proceed with my scheme. Surely, he'd understand I couldn't accept a ride from a stranger, especially since I didn't have too far to walk. How likely was it that a man with his upstanding reputation in a tiny village should have evil intentions, especially a man wearing a black Pierre Cardin trench coat? I decided not too likely.

Dr. Rothgard slipped his hand into a deep coat pocket, brought forth a set of keys, and dangled them before my eyes. "It's the gold, old-fashioned one."

Really angry now at his arrogance, I snatched the keys and gingerly stomped up the porch. The gold key fit perfectly; the ornate knob swung easily; and I pushed open the heavy door. The man was obviously trustworthy, but I still had to get rid of him, before he asked too many snoopy questions. Tomorrow, he'd probably have a moral fit and report me anyway, but why should I care? I'd be long gone.

Dr. Rothgard came up the stairs behind me. "Now then," he said. "Am I redeemed?"

"Maybe," I said, hoping levity would hasten the situation. "You haven't treated me yet."

"So, I haven't," Dr. Rothgard said, as he removed the keys from the lock and re-pocketed them, his eyes never leaving my face. Was he smiling or sneering? "But I soon shall."

I started to follow Dr. Rothgard into the mansion, but he raised a hand. "Wait here," he said. "No need for a second mishap. I will bring a light."

The darkness swallowed him in one gulp, and his footsteps faded into silence. The night was strangely still, and I wondered how late it now was since even the insects had ceased their chirping. The old gray stone building, with its hanging shutters and leaning porch, was the ideal setting for a horror movie, but only because of its remote location and poor condition, for I was still not afraid, only annoyed at this interruption in my plans. I knew ghosts did not exist and even the slim possibility of getting really hurt on the neglected estate had disappeared now that someone familiar with it was keeping me company, not that I'd share that piece of information when I returned to the other girls. A chill shuddered through me as the pre-dawn air cooled around me. I pulled my jacket collar over my neck and wished it was warmer. Perhaps, after the doctor had mended my wounds, I'd head for the broken-down gazebo. It might be less drafty than spending the rest of the night in the open. A white cat slipped around the mansion's corner. I blinked, but the creature was gone. Had I imagined it? Then I heard a meow, but it was only the creaking of the old floor. A wafting light sliced through the blackness. Dr. Rothgard had returned, carrying a long, taper candle in one hand and a cloth bag in the other.

"Follow me," he said, handing me the bag, "and keep this on your nose."

Dr. Rothgard turned left and led me into a room at the front of the house. I meekly placed the ice pack on my nose and shuffled after him. I wondered for a quick moment where he had gotten ice in this broken-down, forsaken place, then foolishly decided good doctors simply came prepared to do their jobs in all circumstances. I sneezed twice under my ice pack as I entered the room, then saw why. Thick dust smothered the parlor carpet, heavy curtains, upholstery, and the curved, wooden legs of the many chairs and tables. Lacy cobwebs swathed the silver picture frames, the blue vases on the mantle, and the pink bric-a-brac. Dust webs hung in long strands from the oil lamps, like tinsel on a Christmas tree. Dr. Rothgard gestured to a two-seater couch near the fireplace.

"Sit down," he said.

"On that dirty thing?" I began, until I remembered my ruined clothes. Two hundred dollars at Miss Emmaline's Boutique, gone. My zeal for spending the night at a reputedly haunted mansion had faded. I was bone tired and eager to get the examination finished as quickly as possible. Wearily, I dropped onto the couch. I couldn't wait to curl up somewhere, anywhere, and go to sleep.

Dr. Rothgard squatted in front of me. "Slip off your shoes."

My shoes? Why my shoes? It was my nose that was bleeding. For the first time since I had run off, I hesitated. My confidence at outwitting Dr. Rothgard was ebbing. Somehow, I had lost my advantage over him. Perhaps, I never really had it? I clenched my toes, for he must not see my shaking and think he intimidated me. Then, I caught a lingering scent of fine pipe tobacco, and I relaxed. He didn't stink of cigarettes like my parents did. Inwardly, I scolded myself. I had allowed the combination of fatigue, the room's eeriness, and local legend to overwhelm sound judgment. Dr. Rothgard had seen it hurt to walk. He was just being a doctor; that was all. I pried away first one shoe, and then the other. He picked up my left foot. I winced, but did not pull away. Beginning with the toes, Dr. Rothgard pressed gently all over my foot, ending at my swollen ankle.

"Nothing's broken," he said, "only sprained."

He repeated the process with my right foot, and I relaxed. He was simply a harmless country doctor. I should be thankful for his help. Why spend the rest of the night unnecessarily hurting? How victorious would I look in the morning, bruised and banged up? Dr. Rothgard moved the ice pack to my swollen hand.

"Hold it here," he said.

With easy, practiced fingers, Dr. Rothgard felt along the bridge of my nose and down both sides.

"Nothing's broken," he said, "and the bleeding has finally stopped. You don't want to do that here, you know. It's very dangerous."

I nearly laughed aloud. Who really was the gullible one? "It's dangerous to bleed? In this mansion? Don't tell me you believe the ghost legend, too!"

Dr. Rothgard stopped, fingers resting lightly on my cheeks, and looked sharply at me. "Do you take me for a fool? Haven't you realized you're miles away from the nearest hospital!"

Before I could retort, he placed his hands firmly on each side of my neck. "Does this hurt?"

An odd twist, a paroxysm of pain, a loud snap, and the wildly spinning room sucked me into a swirling tunnel of darkness. Giant falcons ripped through curtains of black and encircled me.; razors pecked at me; jaws clamped my leg, but as I kicked the large, black beetle, a snake wrapped around me and stared up with glowing, yellow eyes. Another doleful wail and an emaciated form floated past, swiping the air with clawed, skeletal fingers. A platform raised, and thousands of white cats in black choir robes stood and screamed. Moaning wisps melted in hoary, dripping streams. Miles ahead, a bright light blinked, then vanished. I tumbled down, down, down and landed with a hard thump. Four hands lifted me up and moved me through dripping water and moldy dampness. The light grew closer. Identical angels froze in various postures. Hundreds of candles winked their greetings. Was this heaven?

"She's waking," Dr. Rothgard said behind me.

A siren rang. Red lights flashed. The medic on my right was tall with long, blond hair and looked as if he hated the world. The second attendant had dark hair and a slight build.

"What happened?" asked the first.

"She fell," his companion replied.

The door shut, and the ambulance squealed into the night. An intravenous needle poured bloody fluid into my neck. I squirmed against the pain; two hands pushed me back and held me in place.

"My neck," I moaned. "It hurts."

"You mustn't speak," the dark-haired paramedic said, with a warning glance at his co-worker.

I closed my eyes and settled into their care. For once in my life, I felt genuinely thankful for help, for loving friends, and for hospitals. The local idiots would blame my misfortune on the ghost. Well, I would worry about that later. Maybe, I could concoct a story about a band of vicious....

A hard jerk. My eyes flew open. A thermometer slid into my mouth. A cuff wrapped around my arm. A tube slipped past my nose and into my throat. I raised my eyes to the mirror above and saw my battered and swollen face. My worried parents hovered over me.

"You had us so scared," my mother quavered, rubbing my arm and trying to smile through her tear-streaked face. Her pancake makeup had cracked in several places; a false eyelash was halfway peeled off. Despite her tangerine Pucci pantsuit and platinum bleached hair, my mother looked old.

My father, his own Pierre Cardin trench coat, beige, unbuttoned and crumpled, patted my head as if he would never stop. His toupee had slid over one ear and his gray mustache quivered. "Thank God, you're all right!"

Well, God had nothing to do with it, and I tried to tell them so, but my voice wouldn't utter a single syllable. I glanced at the machine on my left. A single line moved across it. I opened my mouth to scream. That's when I realized I wasn't breathing, not one single breath. I bore down hard, but my chest muscles didn't budge. Yet, my parents still smiled benignly at me.

"What would we have done without Dr. Rothgard?" my mother said.

"Yes, what could we have done?" my father echoed.

Dr. Rothgard?

The doors flew open, and Dr. Rothgard, clad in green scrubs, strode into the room. He was real?

"No!" I shouted, but no sound passed my lips. I tried grabbing my mother's sleeve, but my arm wouldn't work. Please, I silently begged her. Please, don't let him do anything to me. Please, make him go away.

She must have noticed my distress, for she smiled encouragingly at me. "It's all right," my mother said. "You just need a little transfusion."

A transfusion? So, I wasn't dead, after all? Would a transfusion restore my heartbeat? Could it make me breathe? Was this normal hospital procedure? A musky-scented mask slipped over my nose, and a white cat scampered out of the room.

"One got away," my father said, smiling.

"That's all right," Dr. Rothgard said. "There's more."

Beyond me were hundreds of beds. On each bed lay a white cat. Tubes poured red fluid from them into me. Was that *cat* blood? I looked up at the mirror. My nose had shrank and turned pink. White fur sprouted on my cheeks. Laughter rang in my ears, and I spun around. One of the pirates pointed and said, "Aw, I told you it was her."

The gorilla nodded and shoved another handful of potato chips between his rubber lips.

I ran the back of my furry hand across my dripping forehead and seriously considered changing out of my costume. The bright yellow and orange walls reminded me of summer campfires, except the colors hurt my eyes and made them water. I pushed through the apple bobbing line toward the snack table. No one else seemed to mind the heat, but then, no one else wore a fur-lined cat costume. *God, it was hot*! I hoped the ice chest was full.

Sitting at the round game table at the far end of the room, just past the food and beverage area, was my friend Melissa. She was wearing a faded Victorian gown and playing cards with a caped figure opposite her. I grabbed two handfuls of ice and rubbed them across my face and along my neck. The ice instantly melted under my scorching skin, but I felt slightly cooler. If only my neck didn't throb so much.

I wandered to the card table and peered over the caped form's shoulder at the cards, and the figure turned. There was no one inside that cape, no one at all. I gasped and woke up.

Dr. Rothgard had pulled up a chair beside the couch and was sitting, watching me and contentedly puffing on his pipe. The fireplace crackled high. I pushed away a blanket and started to sit, but my head pounded and whirled. Queasy, I settled back into the seat cushions and heard the chiming tinkle of a piano. Some else was here, too? I looked at Dr. Rothgard. "Who's playing the piano?"

He lowered his pipe and listened for a long minute. "I don't hear anything."

Dr. Rothgard lowered a green sprig with fuzzy gray-green, heart-shaped leaves over my face. It had the same heady, musky smell as the hospital mask. As I blissfully inhaled it, my lungs expanded and contracted. *I was breathing*! I panted with delight.

"How so you feel?" Dr. Rothgard asked.

"Very strange," I said, still happily huffing and puffing. "Weak, and yet...."

"And yet...what?" He moved the greenery closer, and I swiped it. Quickly, Dr. Rothgard moved it out of reach. The piano notes scurried up then crept back, like tiptoeing mice.

"I feel strangely invigorated."

"Hmmm." Dr. Rothgard dropped the plant back into his bag and reached for the ice pack on the floor. "I'll return shortly."

The lovely notes were softer now, yet definitely unmistakable. Dr. Rothgard was obviously covering for someone. I dug my elbows into the cushion and swung my legs off the couch; my head whirled with the effort. The piano played slowed, halting, wistful. I stood still, teetering, wondering if I could remain upright. Dr. Rothgard would return any second. I had to hurry. Gripping the furniture for balance, I tottered into the hall. The music stopped, and I heard footsteps. Sweat rolled down my face. I wasn't ready for him yet. Which way? I waddled to the grand staircase, dropped to my hands and knees, and crept up the hard wood stairs. At the second floor, I scampered around the corner and crouched there, panting for wonderful breath and congratulating myself at outsmarting Dr. Rothgard.

The door to an east-end rooms was ajar. Moonlight filtered through a cracked window and cast pale bands across the carpet. I heard murmuring voices and again saw Melissa, dressed in that shabby Victorian gown and walking, trancelike, across the room. I softly called her name, but she did not answer. So, I rose to follow her.

I entered the parlor just as she settled on the couch. A tea tray materialized on the sidebar next to me. I poured a glass of water for me and a cup of tea for my friend. A skeleton sprang up, snatched away the items, and gave the tea to Melissa. She raised the cup to her lips. It was filled with blood.

I leaped onto the couch just as the skeleton, teeth bared, was leaning forward to bite her. Melissa choked and blood splattered onto her dress and across the skeleton's face. A bony arm slammed me to the floor; my head banged against a kitchen cabinet; and my fangs sank into a huge rat.

The free-floating parlor dust swirled in the early morning light like a gentle snowfall. I shivered and pulled up the afghan. The fire was out. Dr. Rothgard's head flopped over the back of his chair. I cautiously stretched each limb, but nothing hurt anymore, except my neck, and that only felt stiff, not sore.

Dr. Rothgard grunted and snorted. His eyes fluttered open and immediately rested on me. He leaned forward and motioned for me to come closer. "Let's take a listen to you."

I obediently slid to the edge of the couch and sat quite still as Dr. Rothgard listened to my heart and lungs. When he had finished, Dr. Rothgard looked at me long and hard.

"Well," he said. "You look better. How do you feel?"

"Rested," I said, but I immediately knew that was the wrong word. "Rejuvenated."

Dr. Rothgard smiled, but it was a sardonic half-smile. I couldn't tell if my answer pleased him or not. He replaced the stethoscope, snapped the medical bag shut, and rose. "You're positive you don't want a ride?"

"No," I said, still feeling wary. Last night's dream hung heavy around me.

"Please yourself," he said. "I don't suppose there's any danger, now that it's day."

"Then I'm free to go? You won't try to stop me?"

"Of course you're free to go," Dr. Rothgard said scornfully. "You always have been."

I backed away, toward the door, expecting him to hamper my escape, but Dr. Rothgard was poking around the fireplace, making sure no embers remained. I fled to the front door, flung it open, and bolted down the steps. Without a single look back, I flew across the estate into the thicker part of the woods. It would take me longer to return this way, but it would be impossible for Dr. Rothgard to track me. Yet, he didn't seem to care I had left. Why should he? Obviously, the horror of the previous night was the result of my overactive imagination. I laughed aloud, triumphantly. I had survived the night. I couldn't wait to gloat and receive the lauds due me. I had one over the villagers. Cowards!

The early morning chatter contrasted with last night's stark silence. I never knew woods could be so noisy, low groaning mixed with the clacking of jaws, along with cawing, chirping, and cooing. Even the tweeting of the birds that had not flown south for the winter was deafening. Lake Munson hungrily lapped the shore. Men murmured quite close to my ears, yet I saw no one. A giant rabbit roared past me, and I stood motionless until my racing, thumping heart calmed down. I was more overtired than I thought, but that was easily fixed by napping later this morning, on the drive back to Grover's Park. Trees towered overhead, much higher than when I had first ventured into the woods. Dried foliage swished against my waist and tangled around my burning ankles and knees. I smelled strong coffee and the warm, buttery scent of Brian's toast, comforting reminders of imminent safety. I swayed and dug my heels into the ground, but they would no longer support my weight. The clearing was ahead. The servant's cottage was in full view. I had made it back, just as I had hoped, but it was too late. With a little cry, I dropped to the ground and ran the rest of the way on all four white paws.

END

www.ingramcontent.com/pod-product-compliance
Lightning Source LLC
Chambersburg PA
CBHW071229130626
46555CB00004B/1907